Hysteria 10

Winning short stories, flash fiction and poems from the
Hysteria 2023 Writing Competition

Edited by Linda Parkinson-Hardman

Hysteria 9

Published by: Crystal Clear Books

ISBN: 978-1-7394272-2-1

Website: www.hysteriawc.co.uk

Cover Image: Photo 161701608 | Magician Top Hat © Evgeniy Parilov | Dreamstime.com

ABOUT THE HYSTERIA WRITING COMPETITION

Hysteria is an annual, international writing competition. It opens on the 1st of April each year and closes at midnight on the 31st August. You can find out more about the competition, including rules and guidelines for entries on the website: *www.hysteriawc.co.uk.*

Dedication

The competition and this anthology wouldn't have been possible without the support and help of a wonderful team of readers and this year's writer in residence:

Diane Jackman, Rachel Angel, Steven Patchett, Sharon Boyle, Heather Cook, Sally Curtis, Keely O'Shaugnessy, Yvonne James, Abigail Ottley, Amberleigh Park, Adele Evershed, Alice Penfold, Daisy Blacklock, Kate Franklin, Richard Teague, Gillian Scholey, Malina Douglas, Sally Anderson, Pat Good.

FOREWORD

Words, and the language they make up are, I believe, the most powerful tools we have at our disposal. The way they are used to understand and experience the world is a minute by minute work of creative magic dressed up to look like 'ordinary' life. But ordinary this alchemical reaction is not.

The stories, flash fiction and poetry submitted to this years' Hysteria Writing Competition is linguistic alchemy at its very best. We all know a picture paints a thousand words, and the job of a writer is to weave their words into a picture the reader can see in their mind. And yet, every single picture created in the many minds which read these exception pieces, will be different, because we are all different.

It is through the magic of words, pulled together into sentences and paragraphs, that we can begin to build a different picture of the world we live in.

Savour the texture of the words and language used by each writer in this volume. Take time to see the world through their eyes, and then contrast that with the way you see the world through yours, notice the difference, if there is one. Read it a second time to see if it impacts you differently this time around; what pictures are created in your head? Ask yourself why the work created this picture rather than another, and then reflect on all that brings us together rather than that which strives to pull us apart.

Good writing stands the test of time, if you let them each one of these pieces of alchemy will stay with you long after you have closed the book and put it, for a time, on your bookshelf.

Linda

4

Contents

READERS ADVICE TO ENTRANTS

The Hysteria Writing Competition is supported by a team of volunteer readers for each category. Their role is to read and assess each entry based on a common set of guidelines and questions. They are all writers in their own right, many have won awards and competitions, and between them they bring a wealth of experience about what works and what doesn't. Each year I ask if they would like to share some feedback for entrants about how to enter competitions, common pitfalls and problem areas. Below is a selection of the advice I've received this year.

You can remind yourself who the reading teams were on the website: hysteriawc.co.uk/hysteria-readers-2023/

Reader's Advice for Entrants from Gillian Scholey

When Entering a Writing Competition:

1. Think of at least four ideas linked to the theme of the competition, and go with the fourth. Your first few ideas are likely to be quite obvious links and therefore many people will have chosen them. Judges like originality. Think outside the box.

2. Don't try to be too clever. Your entry should be like an onion. A somewhat obvious exterior but layers of meaning underneath.

3. In a poem, every word must earn its place.

4. Avoid cliches and well known similes/metaphors. Be original.

5. Read the rules and keep checking them. You don't want your work to fail at the admin stage before it even has a chance to be judged for its intrinsic worth.

6. Invest in a thesaurus but use it with care. For example, don't use an archaic word in a modern piece.

7. Be consistent. Check your pronouns and your verb tenses.

8. When writing prose, avoid giving characters similar names. It can be confusing.

9. Read your work aloud and if possible record it. It will help you with the flow.

10. Give yourself time to write your work and put it away for a week. When you return to it with fresh eyes, you will spot your weak points.

Readers Advice for Entrants from Pat Good

I enjoyed reading the entries for the Hysteria 2023 short story competition. While this year's theme of 'magic' was interpreted in a variety of ways, for me, some stories were predictable, and some were a little weak overall.

A piece of advice I've found useful when writing to a theme is to discard the first and second ideas that occur to you. Apparently, these often fall into the commonplace or uninspiring categories. Taking a bit more time with the theme may produce something that stands out from the other entries. Personally, I find themes challenging, so well done to not only those writers who have been placed in the competition, but also to everyone who took the time and effort to enter.

Another tip I find useful is to read my work out loud or use the 'Read Aloud' tool available in some word processing packages. Hearing the words spoken mean I pick up on punctuation errors and catch missing or repetitive words. I often add or take away a sentence to enable the piece to flow more naturally.

If time allows it's a good idea to leave your work aside for a few days, then re-read it with fresh eyes and perhaps give it a final polish.

Finally, I would add, keep writing and good luck with future submissions.

Readers Advice from Adele Evershed

One of my tips for the poetry category would be to read it out loud. That is what I did as a judge. Straight away you can feel if the rhythm is off. You might need a very simple edit use 'it is' instead of 'it's' to give you that extra syllable that will give the piece cadence. It's also s good way to weed out repetitions that don't work- obviously the use of religion can be very powerful but this only works if the repeated word is imbued with power rather than using we or would five times!

Also in poetry you need the language to excite the reader employ all the senses, brainstorm unique metaphors, or use well known sayings in a fresh way. For example 'she fell for him like meat off a bone.'

Collect interesting words or phrases- if you have a few minutes free read an online thesaurus. In fact play around with the words in your poem by substituting synonyms or antonyms- you never know what interesting angles that will throw up.

Readers Advice from Richard Teague

Clarity, spellcheck, editing and typesetting are really important. It's discouraging when you have to read a piece which is very densely arranged in terms of spacing, lack of paragraphs etc.

I would also encourage writers to use the theme in an unexpected way, not a literal interpretation, otherwise the reader has to contend with a sameness in the stories.

I think readers like to be surprised.

Readers Advice from Abigail Ottley

In the poetry section, I would say this. Look for a fresh slant on the theme if there is one and, if there isn't, avoid images and tropes that may already be tired and over-used. Also make sure that your language is fresh and exciting. Surprise and delight the reader. Allow your own poetic voice to be heard. Nothing succeeds like authenticity.

Readers Advice from Heather Cook

I'd like to stress the importance of double checking spelling, grammar and punctuation before submitting entries. The errors seemed to be careless rather than a failed attempt to use an obscure word or challenging sentence construction.

In a short piece like Flash Fiction, it's particularly important to use repetition effectively, possibly as a satisfying end to the story. Overuse of a pet phrase weakens the power of the piece and is a waste of words.

Readers Advice from Sally Anderson

Page numbering and 'THE END' on the final page helps readers know they have read everything submitted, and the entry number at the top of the page is also helpful. As in your advice to writers, the quirky, shorter entries were more appealing than sad tales detailing every step of a bleak journey.

Readers Advice from Sharon Boyle

Writing flash needs a very particular set of skills. We know every word has to work hard in flash, as do titles – in fact, titles are a godsend when the word count is tight; they can act as an extension of the main story. Like poetry, there is scope to play around with line breaks, white space and punctuation. There's a whole lot of thinking going on behind the scenes and yet the story on the page must be seamless.

When a competition is themed, such as this year's Hysteria's, write down all the ideas that the theme offers. Some people suggest not opting for the most obvious idea because you can bet many others will be writing about that too, but it's not only what you choose to write about but the way you write about it. So don't be afraid to pick the one that appeals. The most common or hackneyed idea can sparkle when treated with ingenuity, imagination and intensity. Good luck.

Readers Advice from Sally Curtis

At a writing festival last year, I attended a breakfast for writers of flash. Many of the attendees were new to flash and believed that, because there are so few words to tell the story in, you must let the reader know exactly what has happened to whom, by whom and under what circumstances right at the beginning otherwise they won't understand the story. Nothing could be further from the truth.

Effective flash begins as close to the action as possible, sometimes in the thick of things, sometimes at the end. Very rarely have I read a flash I loved which gives me a complete background and then takes me chronologically through the events from beginning to end. Rather, flashes which throw me into a character's life right now and then work in the relevant parts of their history are the ones I really enjoy.

Readers of flash are a breed who can create the backstory, fill in the gaps, and understand what is going on under the surface without exposition. They can infer your character's past and understand how events might have shaped them without being explicitly told. They enjoy piecing together what they are reading, almost like solving a mystery, often with multiple readings as each read reveals more layers and adds to the overall understanding. It is the nuances of dialogue, action, setting which enables the writer of flash to communicate the mood and message of their writing.

One of the best pieces of advice I received about writing flash was to trust your reader and only tell them what is necessary – they will do the rest for you.

FLASH FICTION

The Flash Fiction category is open to entries with a maximum word count of 250 words. These ultra-short stories needed to be complete and give the reader the satisfaction of not being left hanging.

Flash fiction is fictional work of extreme brevity that still offers the author and reader the benefit of character and plot development.

The overall category winner for the Flash Fiction category was Hocus Pocus by Chris Cottom

HEDERA

Melanie Barrow

Not long now. I smell their lust for the sacrificial hunt, see their faces contorted by the torches' hungry flames, hear their plainsong, 'Burn the Witch.' Yet once they travelled from afar to seek Hedera's knowledge.

I live alone with Quark, my pet toad, for company. I plant chamomile and cumin by the waxing of the moon, and burdock and dandelion when it wanes, infusing the tools of my trade with water from the clear-running river. Henbane and hemlock I give for tired joints, comfrey poultices for broken bones, crushed rue leaves to dispel headaches. With sage, I cleanse their bodies of venom and pestilence.

He came one day, striding across the humped-back bridge, his gold belt glinting in the sun's rays, his surcoat the colour of oak leaves. But my herbals failed me, weren't strong enough to cure the lump I found deep in my lady's womb, nor the lump which grew in my heart as I stared into grey-blue eyes misted with tears. They buried her by the old yew tree and in his grief, he pointed at me.

And so they come, their clogs drumming a beat to chants of suspicion. I drink my potion. My corn-coloured locks tangle into twisted vines and I splinter into clusters of shiny green heart-shaped leaves. I entwine myself around their legs, dragging them beneath the fast-flowing river. My tendrils cling to the bridge, fibres curling, and I creep towards my love.

Melanie studied music at Trinity College, Cambridge and lives in Devon. She began writing fiction during her recovery from long covid and spends every spare minute researching and writing. She won 2nd prize in the Ottery Literary Festival, has been shortlisted for the Wells Literary Festival and longlisted in the Creative Ink writing competition. She's had fiction published in Yours Fiction, Syncopation Literary Journal, Secret Attic, Spillwords, Anansi and non-fiction in The Lady and Best of British. Melanie is currently working on her first dual time fiction novel.

www.twitter.com/WordvilleMel

HOCUS POCUS

Chris Cottom

Rabbit

Dad puts an upside-down top hat on my lap. Inside is a nibbly bunny.

'Hello,' I say. 'Can I call you Hocus Pocus?'

Indian rope trick

'We'll get a takeaway,' Dad says. 'Mum's tied up at work. She's got a new assistant, Anil.'

Dove

Mum's in a flutter, getting ready for a night out with Auntie Pam. I bring Hocus Pocus inside to show him her sparkly dress.

Card tricks

Dad pulls a fan of cards from Mum's purse. 'Hey Presto! No wonder we're overdrawn.'

Cage escape

Mum finds Hocus Pocus in next door's garden. 'He's had an adventure, the lucky thing.'

Vanishing coin

Sometimes Mum borrows my pocket money when she doesn't have enough.

Find the lady

Mum isn't in her room when I need her in the night. In the morning Dad says she's stayed at Auntie Pam's.

Magic carpet

I fall asleep on the rug and feel better when I wake up, although Mum still isn't back.

Sawing in half

Mum says she's going to live somewhere else. With someone else.

'Auntie Pam?'

'No, someone from work. Anil.'

I run outside to see Hocus Pocus.

Mindreading

Dad comes to find me. 'You can go with her, if that's what you want. You and Hocus Pocus.'

Hocus Pocus has magical powers. He's taught me to understand rabbit thoughts.

I put my ear against his soft, warm head.

'He's decided,' I say. 'He likes it here.'

Chris Cottom lives near Macclesfield, England, and once wrote insurance words. This year his stories have won the Allingham Flash

Fiction Competition, National Flash Fiction Day New Zealand's Micro Madness competition, the South Warwickshire Literary Festival Writing Competition, The Phare's Flash Dash competition, and the Off the Rails 3 Minute Story competition (for stories to be read to passengers on the Esk Valley Railway between Middlesborough and Whitby).

@chriscottom.bsky.social

Rescuing A Dryad

Frances Gapper

Last time council workers savaged the rare tree outside our house with their chainsaws, my wife collapsed in the hallway. Another bout of hellish illness: the pupils of her bright fish-darting eyes shrank to Xs, her scalp moulted dead leaves and patches of her bark fell off. Panicking I called for help, but the GP and ambulance service were prioritising humans over hybrids. So having nailed one of her long earrings to the tree and recited a spell, I wooed experts and got a preservation order. Now she can stand unaided, her hair is growing back. She's survived the chop.

Frances Gapper's stories have been published in three Best Microfiction anthologies and online in places including Splonk, Wigleaf, Twin Pies, Trampset, 100 Word Story, Fictive Dream and New Flash Fiction Review. Her three flash and story collections are In the Wild Wood, The Tiny Key and Absent Kisses. She lives in the UK's Black Country.

www.twitter.com/biddable sheep

JUST LIKE GRAN

Angharad Hill

IEveryone said I was just like Gran. And Gran was good at all sorts. Finding lost things. Sorting trouble.

Once, she told me how she did it – how twice a year she'd walk the parish gathering up the greenest nettles, or the juiciest, ripest sloes. Whatever she found went into the ink-pan. Long purples. Hedge-maidens. Millstream water.

She used the finished, grainy ink to write it all down. Everything that needed solving. 'Dunk the paper in your tea until the words dissolve. Then, when you drink, the knowledge comes. It quickens inside you. The answer. You'll know. Only never swallow the paper, you understand?'

She thought I was like her. Good. But I wasn't when it came to John. No, I was wild for Johnny Haskins, for his solemn looks and moon-pale hair. When I saw them together, Flora and John, my rage grew ripe, as keen as nettles. I wrote it down. I drank my tea, then ate the paper, gorging on it till my belly griped and my lips were stained a poisonous sloe-blue.

I rinsed the teapot in the millstream. The dregs held there a moment, a circle of spells, before the current swept on.

Nobody blamed me when Flora was found in the millpond, hair snaking and coiling. Nor when Johnny went off to the Front. Gran was dead, herself, by Christmas. They found her teacup at her feet, and a paper, with my name in ink, only half dissolved, on the point of her tongue.

Angharad Hill is a writing teacher with an MA in Creative Writing from the University of East Anglia. She lives in Dorset. She's an aspiring novelist, represented by Molly Ker Hawn of The Bent Agency, but in 2023 she began experimenting with flash fiction as exercise for one of her writing classes. She was surprised by how much she enjoyed the tight focus and extremely limited word count. Her second effort was shortlisted for the Westword Prize. Her shortlisted Hysteria entry was her first ever attempt at flash fiction.

DUNGEONS AND DRAGONS

Denny Jace

Tommy dropped his plastic car in the forest as soon as he realised that the magician holding his hand was a bad man. Fear set as stiff as custard, solid inside his chest.

The magician had waved a magic stick in front of Tommy's wide eyes, told him about the baby dragons he had at home in his shed. Tommy wanted to see, to touch, to hold, but as they walked Tommy heard the crack of the magic stick under the man's big boot.

Tommy began to cry for his Daddy. The bad man picked him up, hung him over his arm like a sack then clamped his meaty hand over his mouth. Tommy couldn't breathe, he gasped through snot and tears. Around them the breeze teased the leaves on the giant oak trees. The birds and foxes held their tongues as Tommy sunk his teeth into the bad man's hand.

In the darkness the search party marched on tirelessly, their torches seeking and their dogs hunting. Uniformed officers, and village folk swept away bracken with sticks and heavy boots. Two hours in they took a break, sipping from steaming flasks, whispering of lost hope. But one man didn't stop, he trudged through the navy folds of night. He searched until under a soggy dock leaf he found a small plastic car. He doubled over, winded with the force of relief. He picked up the toy, soiled and sodden, and hid it inside the bandage of his wounded hand.

Denny Jace lives on a farm Shropshire with her husband, dogs, cats and tortoise. and has been writing Flash Fiction since 2019. She has just started work on her first novel. Her stories have won and listed in Retreat West, Lightbox Originals, Earlyworks Press, Cranked Anvil, Grindstone Literary, Doris Gooderson, Farnham Fringe Festival, Mslexia, Writers Bureau, Strands International, Henshaw, Bridport Flash, HISSAC and NAWG. Published in Ellipsis Zine, Capsule Stories, Bath Flash Fiction, Reflex Fiction, Oxford Flash Fiction, Cabinet of Heed and Writer's Forum magazine.

www.twitter.com/dennyjace

A TISANE OF THAUMATURGY

Caroline Jenner

The colours were bewitching: pink and white petals suspended on tawny liquid; yellow seeds and golden pollen; tightly knotted red berries peeking from beneath fan-shaped leaves.

"Shall I strain it?" Her hand lay cool against his brow. She looked at him, the town apothecary, weak and shrivelled in his bed; watched him read her lips and nod; wondered how desperate his family must have been to call on her, allow her access to his home, his bed chamber. Slipping from the back door she watched the sun sink, crepuscular light filtering through a mackerel sky; a sense of foreboding shivered down her spine. She knew it would not be long before they came for her.

The apothecary recalled the hue and cry as she fled, bare foot, long hair escaping from her kerchief; he remembered the accusation, pointless to deny, her eyes on his as they lit the faggots beneath the pyre. He recollected the beauty of the infusion, the smell of Chamomile, Echinacea, Feverfew, Goldenseal, Ginko; its scent of well-being.

As the flames licked her skirts he hoped she read his lips, heard his silent thanks for her healing infusion.

Caroline Jenner, a retired English teacher who lives in South London, enjoys writing Flash Fiction and exploring the concise nature of a complete story in a few words. Her work has been published by Free Flash Fiction, Sweetycat Press, Pure Slush, Trembling with Fear and Syncopation Literary Journal. In 2021 she came second in the

Hastings Writing Room Two Halves Flash Fiction Competition, in 2022 she won the Hysteria Flash Fiction prize and in 2023 came third in the Blandford Forum Rotary Short Story Competition.

THE CURE FOR REASON

Catherine Leyshon

Lyssa's Mother hid her magic in her baby daughter's chubby elbow, figuring it was the last place anyone would look. Then she lay down on the bed next to the cot and breathed her last.

That left Father in charge. A man of icy manners, as neat as a pin, with rules of iron.

Bach provided the soundtrack of their lives in Father's symmetrical Georgian townhouse. Chess before breakfast. Father always won. Dinner time discussions of empiricism with logic problems for desert.

When Lyssa was found reading Practical Magic, Mother's books were boxed up in alphabetical order by surname: Allende, Gaman, Hoffman. That left Compte, Descartes and Popper for Lyssa's bedtime stories.

One night, under the covers, Lyssa's elbow started winking like a firefly.

She went to find Father, sitting at the dining room table, his crisp white cuffs peeping from the sleeves of his good wool suit.

"These lights in my elbow. Are they magic?"

He moved his fork a millimeter to perfect the geometry of his place setting. He remembered how his wife had tried to entangle him in her unreason. "If magic were real, it would be possible to consistently demonstrate its effects under controlled conditions."

Lyssa pointed her elbow at him, willed a spell.

Nothing.

26

Alone in her room, Lyssa developed hypotheses, undertook experiments, forged a secret science out of the feeling in her elbow and her heart.

Father loosened his tie. Swapped Bach for Rachmaninov. Ate ice cream for pudding.

And finally lost at chess.

Catherine was born in Coventry in the English Midlands but has spent her adult life moving further and further west. She writes short fiction from her home in Falmouth, Cornwall. Widely published in the academic world, with three edited collections and dozens of academic papers to her name, she has written short stories for several years but has only recently turned to publishing her fictional output. She has seven short stories and flash fiction pieces published in a variety of outlets. Her stories deal with the foundational themes of love, fear, guilt, redemption, hope and duty. Catherine came third in the Crossing the Tees short story competition (2023), third and long-listed for two pieces of flash fiction for Wildfire Words, and has read her work at the Penzance Literary Festival (2023). She gets her best ideas whilst walking her dog, Treacle.

www.twitter.com/CLeyshonWriter

OFFERINGS

Samantha Palmer

You drive to your hometown wanting to show her the bricks that made you. Putting a hand on her knee, you ask if she's okay. She says she's fine, better now, away from the traffic. You want her to say something about the scenery, how prettily the mist drapes over the hills, but her stare out the window is unfocussed.

You start your tour at the school, show her where you got the scar above your left eyebrow in a fight with Nathan Rose. You remember her rubbing a finger over it on your third date, saying it made you look mean and moody and then kissing you. You move on, talking, telling stories – There's the corner shop where you stole chocolate, the park, your first house.

You leave the tree till last. The objects covering the ground where it grows have increased in number. You remember when marbles and figurines were left around the trunk. Now, there are also the remains of flowers and faded pictures, rain and heat turning primary colours grey. They say it's a magical place you tell her, rumours of witches and strangeness. Over the years people have left their offerings, their hopes, trusting the sacrifice will be enough.

You want her to tell you it sounds like rubbish and laugh, then hug you and ask what you would wish for. Instead, she nods and asks what's next. When she turns around to walk back, you empty your pockets and sprinkle coins amongst the roots.

Samantha is a secondary school teacher from Staffordshire. She is currently working on a novella-in-flash and loves writing flash and micro-fiction. She has been published online, featured in printed anthologies and won competitions in Writing Magazine.

www.twitter.com/goodsuspect

PICKING OVER THE BONES

Rachel Swabey

Rhea gazes out over the boneyard, cradling a pomegranate in grubby hands, bare feet dangling from her perch on the big grey box thing. FOH-TOH-COP-YA. One of the words Mum taught her. MOH-BILE-FONE. TEH-LEH-VISHN. Repeat after me. And she'd described what they did. Tales of impossible magic. Worlds in boxes, information in the air.

'Boneyard' is a before-word too. No bones here. Not the animal kind, anyway. Rhea supposes they call it that because it's like a cemetery for ideas. The stories holding those times together left to rot, too broken to make use of. Flotsam of past lives waiting to be reclaimed by earth that's learned to breathe again, to feast on our fanciful notions.

Rhea comes here to think about Mum. About her world, that she insisted on telling Rhea as though it was important. Maybe it was. Maybe there's wisdom here. Or warnings. Rhea liked those stories. They didn't teach her much about surviving in the real world, but Mum didn't know about that.

Rhea learned about survival with the other scrappy kids in the kindom. Grown-ups were no use, hand-wringing about 'rebuilding'. Not many left now. They didn't notice the new world growing, and they didn't have the heart for it anyway. Rhea never saw any of them skin a rabbit.

She cracks the pomegranate, juice spattering pink on the grey box, holds each seed up to the light then pops it into her mouth, every burst of sweetness releasing its own kind of magic.

Rachel is a mother-of-three and local newspaper subeditor from West Sussex, UK. She has won prizes for her short fiction and poetry with Anansi Archive, Globe Soup and the Steyning Festival Short Story Prize and her work has been featured in anthologies from Fly on the Wall Press, Pure Slush and Mum Life Stories, as well as online at Punk Noir Magazine, Every Day Fiction and FlashFlood Journal, who nominated her for Best of the Net 2021. She's working on her first novel, although can often be found bunking off with sneaky little forays into flash.

www.twitter.com/RaeSwabey

LETTERS AND WORDS FROM THE OCCULT

Jarick Weldon

As usual, the letters and words were misbehaving.

Dan had taken the black leatherbound tome from a shelf and opened it on the library table. The book smelled of musty oldness, of spiderweb-filled attics, of dried bones in ancient coffins. A white label on the spine advised: "133.4 — Occult. Reference Only." A prim librarian looked over nervously from her desk. Dan's Goth clothing, piercings, and book choice seemed to have produced a fight or flight reaction. By all appearances, she was considering flight.

The library would close in twenty minutes, but the letters and words were unrestrained. The b's and d's moved as if parading in front of a mirror, while n's and u's backflipped in delight. Words changed their meanings as he tried to scan the spell. A god wanted to be a dog. Blue hid in a blur. Despair trickled into diapers.

Dyslexia was a pain when you were in a hurry to read something important. He needed to learn the hex today.

"It would be great if this could just stop," Dan said out loud.

"Quiet pl..." came a cut-short admonishment from the librarian.

Suddenly, the b's and d's ceased their vane games, the n's and u's came back down to earth, and ruet words revealed themselves as true.

"Hmm, where did my dyslexia go?"

Expecting another "quiet pl...," Dan looked towards the desk. The librarian was frozen rigid with her mouth stuck in a rictus grin, as if about to say "...ease."

"Oops," Dan said.

Jarick Weldon is the pen name of a writer based in Yorkshire and Galloway. In his other life, he is a medical doctor and scientist. Jarick started story writing as a serious endeavour in late 2022. Since then, he has had several short stories published, and a shortlisting in the annual HG Wells Short Story Competition. He is currently studying for an MA in creative writing. Jarick's particular interests are science fiction, the paranormal, historical myths, and humorous encounters. He has a wife, cats, and an interest in Buddhism.

www.twitter.com/jarickweldon

POETRY

The poetry category sought entries with a maximum of 12 lines, not including spaces or the title. Many of our entries followed a strict rule of either four or five-line stanzas, but a few challenged this convention.

Poetry is a piece of writing in which the expression of feelings and ideas is given intensity by particular attention to diction (sometimes involving rhyme), rhythm, and imagery.

The overall category winner for the Poetry category was A Woman Who Does Not Believe In Spells by Annette Iles.

THE SORCERY OF SCIENCE

Linda Burnett

We dare not sway or nudge or cough. Flocked in dust behind the door
the petrified bones of his last sniggerer swing from rusty gibbet claw.

We barely breathe, just stand and stare. His gnarly hands appear to
polish air in circles over tubes. He measures out, with mouthing lips,
spoons from bottles smeared by greasy fingertips. We watch him drip
a drop of this, a glug of that into his mix, motion us to keep well back
before the final potion, sucked through pipette into Erlenmeyer flask.
A grumbling in the brew, as Bunsen burner sputters under glass. Eyes
devour every crumb, waiting for the crunch. He pokes it with stir rod.
Then: Poufff! A miracle of pinks and blues erupts from roiling depths,
threatening escape from holding tank. We gasp. We are enthralled.
We hail the wizard in the lab, charmed by magic to return for more!

Yorkshire-born former teacher of English and Special Needs, Linda
Burnett now lives in Nottinghamshire. About twelve years ago her
love of reading poetry developed into writing. She won the 2020
Penfro Poetry Prize and the 2021 Walter Swan Poetry Prize, and was
recently shortlisted for the Bedford International Poetry Prize and
the Canterbury Festival Poet of the Year. She has had several poems
published in anthologies and online. Two years ago, she fulfilled a
long-held ambition to complete an MA in Creative Writing at York St
John University with distinction. She is an eclectic reader and
regularly writes reviews on pre-published novels. She continues to

write poetry with her local poetry group and to work on her latest
novel.

DAY TRIP TO WHITSTABLE

Heather Cook

We would burst out of the station,

bags and windbreaks banging into legs,

and straggle through dull streets

the same as where we'd come from.

The Thermos always leaked,

indoor skin would flinch from bracing air,

excited chatter settle into grumbles.

But then the light would change

from grey to shining pearl

as if we'd walked into an oyster shell.

My writing very much reflects ordinary life and everyday experiences, which always seem to me to contain so many remarkable things. I'm retired now, so have more time to read and write poetry, but I have always loved it - I blame my mother! I enjoy attending Woking Writers' Circle and the Write Out Loud poetry group, which provides open-mic opportunities. I have received the most wonderful support and encouragement from both groups. I was delighted to win this year's Frosted Fire Firsts competition; the prize is publication of my poetry pamphlet, Out of the Ordinary. The most important thing to me is enjoying my writing. It is wonderful to be shortlisted in competitions, but appreciation of words and capturing thoughts in my poems mean very much more.

https://wokingwriters.wordpress.com

PIED PIPER

Maureen Cullen

My pied piper sways out of the fog

of misshaped forms

herding along Buchanan Street,

whilst she floats on air

in leather and feather, a tequila sunrise,

skin milky as moonshine,

plump scarlet lips set in total entitlement,

heels now clicking an insistent tune.

Like a child of Hamelin,

I follow the toss of her crested head

through Fraser's mahogany, gold-trimmed doors,

my credit card doing the salsa.

Maureen Cullen lives in Argyll and Bute. In 2015, she was awarded an
MA in Creative Writing (Distinction) from Lancaster University. She
has stories and poems published in a range of magazines. She has a
Poetry Conversation Sherry and Sparkly, with Patricia M Osborne,
published by the Hedgehog Press. In 2021, Maureen was shortlisted

for the V. S. Pritchett Short Story Prize. She has a novel Kitten Heels to be published by Ringwood Publishing in May 2024.

www.twitter.com/maureengcullen

A Woman Who Does Not Believe In Spells

Annette Iles

gathers candles, hawthorn, sets a bowl

on the sill in a certain place so that water

can draw moonlight into its centre

she does not believe in this but is broken

by injections, hormones, scans, the pinpricks

of pity in the consultant's voice   feels herself

shrivelled from a person to a failed procedure

the tides of her body were lunar once, might

this huge-bellied moon hold a child in its gift?

she does not believe, but what is a spell except

a different way of asking?   the woman

opens the window wide   wider

Having grown up in rural New Zealand in the 50s, Annette Iles now
lives in a Midlands village beside the Grand Union canal. She began
writing after she retired, introduced to the delights and challenges of

poetry through an adult education class. Her work has appeared in a variety of magazines and anthologies; in 2018 she won the West Midlands Poetry on Loan competition.

A Kind Of Magic

Iain McGrath

In summer's sluggish sweat
he's centre stage,
microphone stand a wand,
casting spells through
the herbal haze and airwaves
to feed the hungry masses.
Without smoke or mirrors,
just the bewitching charisma of quicksilver,
this bohemian's rhapsody
gains immortality in twenty minutes.
The King of Queen:
Freddie Mercury.

Iain McGrath is retired and writing is his hobby.

https://iainmcgrath.substack.com/

YOKED

Fiona Ritchie Walker

You have knitted me into the north,
unravelled my southern dreaming.

This patterned yoke, such heritage
worn across my shoulders

weaves the dark sky's dancers
deep into the marrow of my bones.

These stitches release a compass,
head south to find me.

See how the city melts away
as I dress myself with home.

Fiona Ritchie Walker is from Montrose, Angus, now based in
Bournville, Birmingham. Her Scottish roots and love of travelling
often inspire poems and short stories. Her work has been widely
published in collections, anthologies and magazines, most recently in
Postbox Magazine, Amsterdam Quarterly and Magma.

www.twitter.com/guttedherring

My EÄRENDIL

Gillian Scholey

Darkness and pain surround me.
Winter infuses my heart and bones,
and alone, eyes closed, I cry the night.
A mote, silver, tiny as an elf's fingernail,
pierces the skin of my swollen eyelid.
Aboard a boat on the blackest of seas,
anchor weighed and steadfast,
floats the holy mariner of the skies,
Eärendil, bearer of the jewelled light.
He refuses to be repelled. Nightlong
he cups my fragile life, buoying me up,
holding me fast, until the tide of morning.

Gillian Scholey is from Cumbria. She loves writing both prose and poetry, and is a member of several writing groups.Gillian has been a Hysteria finalist on several occasions and is now in the midst of writing her first novel. She also hopes to have a poetry pamphlet out in 2024. Gillian has had work published in several anthologies including Morecambe Bay Poetry Festival Anthology, Poetic Vision, Poetry for Ukraine and Epona and the Golden Bees. She has also had work accepted by Reach, Dawntreader and Dreich. Her prose writing is legion and varies in length from six words up to two thousand. When not writing, Gillian tries to persuade her husband to buy a Westie puppy. This is a long running battle!

THE DANGEROUS THIRD WISH

Sue Spiers

What would soldiers do if I wished for world peace?
Munition factories closed and workers on the street.

If everyone was as rich as me (second wish of cash)
would that end poverty or would jealousy persist?

My loved ones made immortal, would they take more risks?
Would good health let me last as long, unforgiven for the gift?

No natural disasters to crush a city's walls,
leave survivors homeless, until the earth implodes.

I could save endangered species: man-eaters and microbes;
scaly beasts and poisoned frogs; all creatures hatched or born.

If I could not wish for wishes and had to pick just one,
I'd choose the leprechaun's idea of what he thought was fun.

Sue Spiers lives in Hampshire and works with Winchester Poetry
Festival. Sue edits the annual anthology for the Open University
Poetry Society and supports Winchester Muse, T'Articulation and
Pens of the Earth groups. Her poems have appeared in Acumen,
Artemis, Dream Catcher, Fenland Poetry Journal, Hysterias 4, 9 & 10,
The North, Prole, South magazines and on-line at Atrium, The High

Window, Ink, Sweat & Tears, The Lake, London Grip and Spilling Cocoa. Sue has worked with artist Nicola Henshaw on the Romsey Canal project and photographer Janey Devine on the City Space project writing poems to compliment art work.

https://twitter.com/spiropoetry

RE: YOUR LOVE SPELL ON OXFORD STREET

Katherine Weber

Hey,

So, I think you cast a spell on me, please find evidence attached. As you can see:

- my eyelashes have turned into spiderwebs, my fingernails are corkscrew
- my tears come out shaped like the letters W, A, I, and T, my exhales are blue

What did you do, you should've disclosed 'magical powers' on your profile,

Catfish, my head detaches and plays hide & seek when I recall the moment we met

I quite literally levitated when I thought about our Pret coffee

I've put an exorcist in the CC (Carrie, I'd be grateful for your insight)

A butterfly climbs out of my mouth everytime I think of you, it's irritatingly sweet...

Jerk. I know you cast a spell on me on Oxford Street, what did you do to me, I can't stop thinking about your alchemy, I –

I can't wait any longer, please, just, set me free –

Katherine is from Virginia, USA. She graduated in 2020 from the University of St Andrews with a degree in English. She lives and works in London and in her spare time she writes poetry and fiction.

https://facebook.com/katherineweber4

TABLECLOTH TRICK

Glen Wilson

Candles make everything a vanilla vignette,
soft music gets in on the act, side plates shine
as our forearms taper on the red and white gingham.
It's our anniversary, yet you haven't touched your wine
only folding and unfolding an off-white napkin
before you interrupt me mid-anecdote - There's someone else.

And the tablecloth is gone by your sleight of hand,
underneath is the worn mahogany, names scratched,
tally marks gouged deep in the wood. The light flickers,
 the bottle of Chianti teeters, knives, and forks tremble
but nothing falls and all I can do is look across the table
at where you once were, a stranger in your place.

Glen Wilson is a multi-award winning Poet from Portadown. He won the Seamus Heaney Award for New Writing (2017), the Jonathan Swift Creative Writing Award (2018), the Trim Poetry competition (2019), and Slipstream Open Poetry competition (2021). He has had poems commissioned by the Irish Football Association and appeared on the Poetry Jukebox. He was runner up in the 2022 Ulster Scots writing Competition and won Third prize in the Ulster Scots category of the 2023 Frances Browne Multilingual Poetry competition. His collection An Experience on the Tongue is available now.

www.twitter.com/glenhswilson

SHORT STORIES

The short story category is for entries of up to 1000 words, not including the title. The short story genre is a staple of writing competitions the world over and many writers will hone their skills in this medium before venturing into the world of longer fiction.

A short story is something that can be read in a single sitting. According to Wikipedia, the written short story emerged from the tradition of oral storytelling in the 17th century.

The overall category winner for the Short Story category was Soaking Wet by Denarri Peters

Skin Deep

Sarah Breen

Did it expect her to feed it? It didn't seem especially hungry. It appeared neither pleased nor agitated.

She wasn't even sure what it was. It looked like a lizard; maybe a bearded dragon. Those things were aggressive, right? No, that was a Komodo dragon. Maybe. She'd look it up later.

She wondered if it could climb. She cursed her past self for scrolling on her phone instead of paying attention during Arthur's beloved nature documentaries. The lizard seemed uninterested in her. A ribbon of black snapped out of its mouth. Her stomach twisted.

Had she screamed? She remembered shuffling to the kitchen, noticing movement nearby, and then she was crouching on the sofa, a pillow in one hand and her phone in the other. In hindsight, screaming seemed so ineffective and besides, who would hear her anyway? That was a bleak thought.

Her security system would have sounded if anyone had entered via a window or door. The garage! It must have slithered under the door and then pushed in through the laundry room.

Goddamnit, Arthur.

She squeezed her eyes closed. No, that wasn't fair. Just because he was the last one to come home the night before didn't mean that this was his fault.

This creature had gained access with the help of someone. Or something.

But that was not what she needed to worry about right now. Right now, there was a three-foot-long reptile in her den.

She didn't feel like she was in danger. Confused? Absolutely. But not terrified. She began laying out scenarios where she would be required to share her abode with this creature, divvying up living space like ex-lovers and agreeing on a schedule for common areas. Did it need to go to the bathroom? Had it already gone?

What if it was pregnant? Oh God, what if it had laid eggs?

She forced in a deep breath. When Arthur got home he would know what to do.

Now that the initial shock had worn off, she took the opportunity to examine it. If it had been on the other side of thick glass in a reptile sanctuary, she would have enjoyed following the interlocking pattern of its scales as they flowed down its back, black fading to gray. Shifting in the sunlight, waves of iridescence cascaded over its form all the way to the tip of its gleaming black tail, sucking up color like an oil spill. Thorn-like claws clacked against the slate tile as it dragged its dry belly, struggling closer to the warmest bit of flooring.

A thin scar cut diagonally between its eyes. Its face did not convey intelligent thought. The more she stared at it, the more enamored she became. Was it glistening?

She blinked. It was sparkling! Alternating shimmers of fuschia and indigo raced along its spine, increasing in speed as if it was charging its lizard batteries. The pulsating movement was accompanied by a low buzz. It ducked its head between its curled paws, completely content. It began to purr.

She dashed into the kitchen and splashed water on her face. She was hallucinating. This entire experience was a hallucination.

When she turned around, the lizard was gone.

Slamming her palm against her breastbone, she wheezed with relief. It was curled up in the recliner, its chin (do lizards have chins?) resting on the chair's arm. Surely, it would claw the leather upholstery. Oh well, that was the lizard's chair now. She would throw it out later. She'd never really liked it but Arthur would be exceedingly upset. If she got lucky, the lizard would climb on the sofa and take a nip out of the misshapen hemp rug they'd been gifted by her cousin.

By now, the animal's shimmering had subsided, now only giving off the occasional flicker.

It didn't seem to be afraid of her. Was it sitting this closely on purpose?

No, it was a lizard. It acted on instinct.

Speaking of, was it hungry?

She set out plates of vegetables she found in the fridge: limp celery, a bowl filled with slimy spinach, an apple of unknown origin, and a clump of frozen broccoli.

If this was going to continue, she needed to get comfortable. Grabbing some cheese puffs and a bag of wasabi peas, she twisted into her corner of the couch.

The lizard perked up at this, its head following the repetitive motion of her hand.

"Want some?" she asked. Its tongue darted out.

"These aren't good for you, you know?" she said. "I'll feel bad if you die from eating this." She flipped the bag to check the list of ingredients, which was difficult with her fingers coated in orange powder and hydrogenated vegetable oil.

Her first toss went long, sailing over the recliner. "Fine," she mumbled, making her arm a pendulum and launching the puff up and onto the lizard's back. A flash of the black ribbon and it was gone.

She ate the puffs, tossing every fifth one toward her new roommate.

Stomach full, exhaustion pinned her shoulders to the sofa, the sound of purring lulling her to sleep.

She awoke to a soft chuffing sound. Something organic, heavy and humid, tinged her nostrils. She tucked her hands, pressing them to her chest, as her thoughts congealed slowly, watery in the center and firming at the edges.

The blanket-covered lump in front of her was human-shaped. But she knew better than to trust her eyes.

The unmistakable sound of Arthur's yawn released a knot of tension at the top of her spine. She blinked her eyes open, finally allowing herself to stare. It was him, his sandy hair spiked and feathered against the pillow.

She pressed her palm to his spine. He was real. This was real.

His hiss pummeled fear into her gut. She snatched her hand back.

This seemed to wake him. He twisted, shaking the sheet off of his shoulder, revealing deeply sunburned skin.

What on earth?

Sarah Breen lives in Berlin, Germany, where she works as a Senior Technical Program Manager. When not chasing deadlines, she is happiest curled up on her sofa with a fantasy or YA novel or texting bad jokes and cute animal videos to her family in America. The encouragement received from her husband and her online writing community spurred her to share her stories with a broader audience. She is in the throes of finishing her first novel, which she plans to publish in 2024.

www.linkedin.com/in/breensarah/

My Darling Boy

Sally Curtis

Because I told him he had a smile as wide as a crocodile, he snaps his teeth when he sees me.

"Don't eat me Mr Croc. I'm here to visit my friend Jaspar. Have you seen him?"

"You're silly, Mabs."

I know him well now and when sleep coaxes others into the land of strange imaginings or blessed nothingness, we talk of secret dens and enchanted gardens, hide from dinosaurs and dragons prowling across the yellowing wall. I know the tricks he can do on his bike, why Mr Brownlow is the best teacher in the whole-wide-world-ever and how he dared his friend Ben to eat a worm and had to give him his Superman figure when he did.

"I've made up a joke for you, Mabs. Knock, knock."

"Who's there?"

"Boo."

"Boo who?"

"Don't cry or the magic might not work."

I laugh and his grin reveals his pride.

"You're right, Jaspar. No feeling sorry for yourself."

"And this time I'll be better, won't I? No more machines."

He has some awareness of the enormity of what is about to happen but he cannot grasp its complexity and so he copies his parents' joy when they speak of their gratitude to a selfless stranger and the miracle match, takes on their unease when they murmur dangerous rhymes like infection and rejection.

I always wait for his parents to pull themselves away from his bedside to grab a coffee or smoke a secret cigarette which Jaspar's mum will pretend she cannot smell on her husband's clothes. Jaspar pretends not to smell it either even though, when his dad kisses him, the staleness reminds him of bad medicine. Tonight they were loath to leave, the nurses ushering them away to another room to feign sleep, his mum's heels click-clacking on the grey linoleum, his dad wondering if he could slip off for one last smoke.

"Do you want to talk about tomorrow?"

Jaspar nods. His blonde fringe falls across his eyes and I brush it away, as I have so many others.

"Tell me what you want to know."

"Will the magic hurt?"

I take his hand, imagining for a moment it is another. "Magic doesn't hurt. Not proper magic. Proper magic makes everything better. One minute, you'll be chattering away and the next, silver sparkles will sprinkle from the sky and take you to all the places we've seen and talked about. When you open your eyes, it will all be over."

"Does it always work?"

"As long as you believe hard enough."

There is no need for him to know sometimes the magic isn't strong enough, or it comes too late, no matter how much you wish it.

"Mab? Will you be there?"

"Of course, my darling."

I stay with him until the sun rises, stealing away before his parents return, their cheerful chatter composed to drown out their fear.

When the time comes, they sit together in a cavernous silence, her twisting her wedding band, him picking at a polystyrene cup, helpless but for their faith in what they have been told.

In theatre, I know better than to get in the way of the doctors executing trusted routines. The taste of sanitation is sharp: disinfectant, soap, detergent. I stand back as nurses and technicians check the monitors, reading the beeps and the blips, following the rise and fall of red and green waves on the screens.

The anaesthetist masks Jaspar's smile and, just before sleep claims him, I slip through and scatter my silver dust. He scrunches his eyes and away he travels to the worlds we created and everyone waits for his safe return.

Between the coming and going of medical staff and his parents, it has been difficult to find him alone since the surgery. Sitting on the edge of his bed is not allowed, but I want to be close and I don't have much time before someone else comes to check on him. He opens his eyes.

"Hello my lovely. Where did you travel?"

"I went to a forest and fought a dragon." His voice is husky. "Did the magic work? Can I go home?"

"You'll need to stay a little while longer but soon you'll be back on your bike, and building dens and telling Mr Brownlow all about it. You might even be able to get your Superman back if you eat a bigger worm."

He smiles. Such small ambitions.

"Will I see you again?"

I never return. They are not my children to love, but this time saying goodbye grieves me. To stay and delight in the reminders and memories Jaspar has re-opened for me of another time, of another boy, pulls me closer to him. I always believed it is I who chooses them but this time I think he chose me.

He frowns.

"What's troubling you, my love?"

"How do I know it really was magic? How do I know it wasn't just the clever doctors?"

"Watch this."

I kiss his forehead and a thousand silver sparkles shoot into the air and with them I am gone.

Sally lives on the south coast of England near the sea and has never moved far from it. She has been writing with intent for the last few years and has been successful in various writing competitions. She is published online by Retreat West, Globe Soup and Fiction Factory amongst others, as well as in various paper anthologies including Reflex Fiction and Scottish Arts Trust. She particularly enjoys micro-fiction and flash although she is now focussing on developing longer stories. She writes all different genres but loves those with a surreal feel. Having recently tried her horror voice she has had two stories published in the Fictional Reality anthology. She enjoys red wine, blue cheese and making people feel better through hypnotherapy and sharing a nice Malbec.

www.facebook.com/sallywritesstories

THE LONELINESS OF ORBIT

Fay Brown

The woman with moonlight in her soul dreams a sombre piano movement. She glitters over still waters, sings a river (wider than a mile). This woman, whose name is Audrey, bathes in the liminal. She watches over spell-casting maidens and the protective magic of hags.

The woman with moonlight in her soul has a sister with sunlight in her heart and they meet rarely, only to obscure the other. Audrey wonders whether this makes her sister sad as well. But her life swings on its axis, beyond the rotundity of their Mother, who is the Earth. In the loving embrace of Father Sky, she is protected from collision with her gently rotating sibling.

The woman with moonlight in her soul watches over lovers and horrors alike, unable to intervene. She loves to walk on midnight snow, when the light of her eyes reflects just so. Love is as unknowable as a handful of light. Much abused by Shakespeare, Audrey is neither unfaithful nor inconstant. She is, in fact, much less fickle than her sister, who skuds about with clouds and shadows (and whose light Audrey has not stolen). She does not pivot close enough to make a man mad.

Meetings good and ill fall under her purview; she has a dark side after all. Who doesn't?

Audrey has been painted before, her quiet smile captured by a master who nevertheless laid down a face unlike her own and granted it an enigmatic name. But imagination couples with nimble minds, and she is no longer a distant witch's round. Heavy boots bounded on her surface, kicking up mineral dust. The remnants of a great dream of Nation clutter her once-pristine curves. Parts of her are named. She has birthed a sliding backwards dance, and the moon-shot is a politician's tool.

A new artist paints the curve of Audrey's pale cheek, inscribes her lambent eyes. He reads space-opera, watches Mars-bound rocket tests, and returns to his easel. He tells her that, one day, men will live on the moon. The artist becomes lost in time and brushstrokes, and the lingering scent of his muse. He calls Audrey and she comes, though most sitters would baulk at the hour. By lamplight he conjures her face. And the woman with moonlight in her soul is quickened. Her heart thrums racing scales of desire. She is seen.

The next night is a new moon, which is lucky because Audrey is too busy to oversee anything.

The woman with moonlight in her soul has three children with her artist; they carry stars in their minds and dream great futures. They dart up into the waiting arms of Grandfather Sky, leaving the great fastness of Grandmother Earth to rest and wonder at their audacity.

Fay is a teacher who lives on the south coast of England. She is often inspired by seafront walks, her geriatric dog, and the things teenagers say when they think you can't hear them. She fell in love with flash and short fiction writing with Writer's HQ during the pandemic and really should get back to redrafting her first novel. Her work can be found at Lucent Dreaming, Propelling Pencil, NFFD 2022 and Fudoki.

fabwrites.bsky.social

A Living Bethlehem

Christine Griffin

It's a fifteen minute walk from my flat to the Mission which is quite a long way when you're dressed as a shepherd complete with crook and carrying two bags of potatoes. No-one gives me a second glance - I'm just another crazy woman to them. Anyway, I'm batting along the High Street when I spot him walking just ahead of me - an Angel complete with massive wings and he's definitely not one of us.

It had been Bob's idea to dress up – he's Melchior by the way - but no-one wanted to be an angel 'cos of the wings getting in the way, so that's how I know the fellow in front isn't to do with us. Next minute he's gone. Oh well. Stranger things have happened. Made me feel a bit spooked though.

Still, there's more important things to think of – like will the guests actually turn up. They say they will but when it comes to it – well you know. As I get to the corner by the mission it starts to snow – big fat flakes and at that moment the church bells began to ring. I feel this kind of fizzing in my stomach that I used to get when I was a child on Christmas Eve. The sound of carols floats from a nearby church. 'O little Town' – one of my favourites. That cheers me up no end. Everything's going to be alright.

Inside, the hall's buzzing. There's a bunch of shepherds getting the veg ready and Melchior is fiddling with the lights on the tree. There's Christmas music on the radio and a delicious smell of roasting meat coming from the oven.

I dump the potatoes in the kitchen and go to have a look round. The trestle tables are out and in each place there's a cracker and a gift-wrapped parcel. I knitted the gifts myself – all year it took me. Twenty woolly hats and twenty pairs of mittens. There's paper chains strung across the ceiling, and fairy lights looped round the windows. This is much nicer than sitting alone in my flat watching the telly. Still, can't stand around gawping. There's work to be done. I roll up my shepherd sleeves and make a start on the potatoes.

By midday a small queue has started to form outside the mission. They're a mixed bunch. We know most of them, though there's always a couple of new ones who've fallen on hard times. They're the ones who usually cry and your heart goes out to them, I can tell you. There but for fortune and all that. We all line up to welcome them in – Joseph, Mary, various shepherds, an innkeeper, the Kings. I'm so glad we decided to be a 'Living Bethlehem' – that's what Melchior called it – and I must admit it's brought a smile to the faces of our guests.

Anyway there we are just about to serve the main course when wouldn't you know it the power goes out. Good job we've finished the cooking is all I can say. I'm just putting out the sprouts when I become aware that everything's gone quiet. And that's when I see him - that Angel fellow I saw in the street earlier.

And then it gets even weirder. Suddenly there's a load more of them – nineteen more in fact all looking exactly the same. Each one of them walks to stand by a guest and places a hand on their shoulder.

To tell you the truth, it was mesmerising. Total silence in the hall, the glow of the fairy lights, snow swirling outside, the church bells ringing. I've never felt such peace in my life and I don't expect I ever will again.

That's when I spot old Corky from the railway arches. He's up from his seat still with the Angel's hand on his shoulder and he's starting to sing. And I'll tell you what – it's the most beautiful thing I've ever heard. He sings 'Silent Night' with the voice of an angel. Magic. Utter magic. I don't mind telling you, it makes me cry.

66

The lights snap on without any warning and everything is as it was. I'm holding the sprouts, Old Corky is eating a roast potato and the other shepherds are plating up the Christmas pudding as though nothing had happened. I wonder if it's just me having a funny five minutes so I say nothing.

We have a lovely afternoon with carols and mince pies but gradually the guests drift away wearing their new hats and mittens. They never stay long – not really used to being inside.

On the way home, I pass under the railway arches and there's a few of them there. They've got a brazier and a Salvation Army wagon is dishing out hot drinks. And now you really are going to think I'm crazy but I swear I can see that Angel fellow in the distance watching.

Back home, I sit by my fire and go over the day. I'm so tired I can't be bothered to change out of my shepherd outfit. The room seems different somehow, but I can't put my finger on it. I pull my chair closer to the fire and that's when I spot it – a big bundle wrapped in Christmas paper. I haven't had a proper Christmas present for years and I have no idea how it got here and who it's from as there's no label. I open the wrapping and a large bundle tumbles out and for a moment I can't believe what I see. It's best quality wool in lovely shades which seem to make my room glow. And you know what? I'm pretty sure I know where it's come from. Expect you can guess too.

I get up and root about for my knitting needles. No harm in making a start. After all, those woolly hats won't knit themselves, will they?

Christine writes poetry and short fiction and has been widely published including in Writing Magazine, Acumen, The Dawn Treader, Wildfire Words and many others, not least in past editions of Hysteria! She belongs to several local groups who all provide inspiration for her writing. She has performed her work at the Cheltenham Literature Festival and the Cheltenham Poetry Festival.

CLAUDETTE

Julie Lockwood Austin

Denise works in Ladies' Accessories. She's in charge of handbags. She started nine years ago, two weeks after her husband left her for the woman treating his fungal nail infection. The job suits her well and just about pays the bills on her tiny flat. The work is simple, if hard. In the evenings, when she rubs the knots out of her calves, she reminds herself that exhaustion means the oblivion of sleep comes more easily. Her colleagues are generally polite and Mr Brown, the manager, praises her sales figures and often exchanges a line or two about the weather. Some of the regular customers appreciate her knowledge of the products. And it is the spell these products have spun over her which keeps her going. The handbags she sells have stolen her heart.

When she can, first thing in the morning, last thing before closing or in the sleepy lull after lunchtime, she'll trail clean fingers across their buttery leather surfaces and worry which of her precious brood she might lose that day. Which one will be picked up, held against a coat or dress, hung over a shoulder, squeezed and poked and then whisked off to begin a new life without her?

"An excellent choice, Madam," she'll say through a twist in her throat. The buyers, with their sharp haircuts ignore her advice on cleaning and after care with bored expressions.

If she could, Denise would buy every last one and look after them all. But even the least expensive is far beyond her means. They are all special — the chic black ones, the sassy reds, the conservative blues, the natural browns and the trendy multi colours. Each one has its own little personality, its likes and dislikes. And only Denise knows what these are. And the smell of them! She can't resist burying her faintly lined face into their softness, filling her lungs with their scent. It is, she believes, the very essence of heaven. Though what alchemy has turned the stench of a slaughtered cow hide steeped in urine to a perfume like that she'll never know. Silk purses, she likes to say, really can be magicked from a sow's ear.

She loves them all. But she has a favourite. And that favourite is a secret. A secret that burns in the bottom of her stomach and has done for several months now. One average morning, she'd arrived at work early, as she always did.

"Good morning, Denise!" said Mr Brown. "A fine day."

She agreed that, indeed, the weather was agreeable.

"There's an order arrived already. Could you...?"

"Certainly, Mr Brown." In the stockroom, she unpacked the handbags from their boxes. There were big bags that could carry almost everything Denise owned, small bags for an evening out, bags with long straps for days idling with friends. Then she unwrapped the last one.

"Oh my!" she gasped.

The bag was pink. The soft, greyish pink like the inside of a new kitten's mouth. It had two perfectly arched handles, a discreet gold logo and an interior the colour of thick cream.

It was hers. It had to be. There was no other way. It could not go into the shop where the eyes of haughty women would linger grubbily over it. She hugged it to her cheek. "I'm so glad I've found you."

The bag looked at her.

"Claudette. I think your name is Claudette," Denise whispered.

"Everything shipshape down there?" Mr Brown called.

70

Denise jumped and banged her elbow on a storage rack. She placed her finger over her lips, "Shh!" she said to Claudette. "Just coming, Mr Brown!" She wrapped up Claudette and placed her behind some boxes at the back of a shelf. "You'll have to be patient. It will be worth it, I promise."

Since then, whenever Denise is in the stockroom she whispers to Claudette. "Not much longer."

One chilly Tuesday morning the rescue plan begins to take shape.

"Good morning, Denise." Mr Brown opens the door. "Winter is on its way."

"A nip in the air," Denise agrees.

"A handbag delivery has arrived. I'll help you."

"No need. I'll manage." He looks disappointed, but she can't miss the chance of time with Claudette.

Denise checks the docket from the supplier – ten bags are listed. Eleven have been delivered. An extra bag! Her insides twirl around on themselves. At last. She can juggle the figures. Claudette will soon be free.

"Nearly home!" She strokes Claudette through the tissue paper.

For the rest of the morning Denise bites back a smile. She even nods at one of Mr Brown's jokes. For the next few weeks, she lets the bags she sells depart with nothing more than a quick pat.

On Christmas Eve, when everyone is preoccupied with a small glass of complimentary sherry, she slips Claudette out from the back of the shelf and pushes her under the festive jumper she's had to wear since mid-November. She wraps her big winter coat around them both.

"Happy Christmas, Mr Brown." She distracts him with a mistletoe peck on his papery cheek.

He puts his hand to the faint lipstick mark. "Denise, I ..."

"Must dash." She ducks out of the door into the slanting rain. Raindrops, sharp as needles, bounce off her, unnoticed. It's going to be a magical Christmas.

The next morning, the bells across town welcome the day. Denise sips coffee with Claudette on her lap. She opens the three Christmas cards she has received. One is from her landlord with a reminder of the coming rent increase, and one is from her ex-husband, the nail lady and their new baby. The last is from Mr Brown. Or Graham, as it says in neat letters. He suggests they meet up for tea on Boxing Day. His treat.

"What do you think, Claudette? Should we go?"

Claudette looks up at her and smiles.

"Gosh!" laughs Denise. "Well, if you think so. Now we're together, everything feels possible."

A LINGERING SCENT

Sarah Masters

Sam tightened his apron strings and inhaled deeply. Nothing. No yeasty scent of the loaves stacked just feet away; no sweet stickiness from the almond croissants that enticed customers on a Saturday; no peppery warmth from the pasties laid out below the heat lamp.

"Sam! Oven!" his boss yelled.

No sour stench of burnt crusts from the oven Sam had forgotten to check.

"Bloody hellfire, Sam. If you can't use your nostrils, set a timer."

They'd have sacked him if they could get anyone else to work here. It was the first place Sam had walked into after the pandemic and they'd hired him on the spot. It was the lethargy that was killing him. Every morning he woke up listless, trudged through the day with not a speck of interest in anything. He envied the customers their appetites, their greed for life, even their rudeness as he tonged sausages into baps, wrapped buns in napkins, kept his head down and waited for his shift to be over.

He wasn't sure what made him look up at this customer, the one in the threadbare coat pressed up against the counter.

"Bread," the man whispered.

"Bread?"

"Any spare bread for my goat?"

"Goat?"

The man unfurled a poster on the counter. Circus, it said in letters of red and yellow flame. He waved a wrinkled finger over the cluster of acts. "Goat whisperer, that's me."

Sam stared at the paper, a vague memory of circuses past breaking through the fug in his brain. But Sam's boss had got wind of the exchange. "Sorry mate, no promotions here," he said quickly. "And no freebies."

The man hunched his shoulders, stuffed his posters back inside his pocket and turned to leave.

The door pinged shut and Sam had a sudden urge to follow him. He grabbed one of the burnt loaves. "Won't be a sec, boss!"

The customer was still outside. Sam held out the loaf. They both stared at its burnt and blackened crust. "For the goat," Sam said.

The man's eyes crinkled. "Well, that's very nice of you." He pulled out a poster with a flourish and pointed. "Pandemonium. That's me. The man with the talking goat. Final date before I retire." He reached behind his ear, pulled out a stub of pencil and scribbled an address, then shoved the poster at Sam. "Meet me at four and I'll have something for you."

Sam endured the rest of the morning, allowing himself to be pushed around by customers and his boss. Like a crumb on the worktop, he thought. Then as the clock rang home time he wound his scarf round his neck and stepped out into the fog.

The carpark on the edge of town had been transformed for the circus. Sam checked the pencilled note and made his way past the giant striped teepee to a plain buff tent where the goat whisperer was waiting for him. Sam had half expected him to be accompanied by his goat, but perhaps it was too precious. Instead, the man pulled the burnt loaf from

74

his pocket, offered it to Sam, then with both hands broke open the crust. "Smell."

Sam pushed his nose towards it and –

was met with such a sweetness as he'd never encountered. The first sniff and he was a child swathed in blankets with the chimes of a mobile playing above his head, the second and his grandmother was beside him stroking his hair, the third and his feet were crushing herbs on a mountain path.

He awoke having slept the most delicious, the most enveloping sleep. His head felt clear. He remembered how it felt to be alive, to love, to desire. He turned over, and felt some resistance. He looked down, and noticed that his foot was tethered to something. He followed the rope to a chain that disappeared under straw. He peered around him with interest. In the gloom it was hard to make out anything except the vast space above him.

There was a slap of tarpaulin and the old man appeared. In his arms was a bundle of sheepskin. "Now then, Sam" he crooned. "You've had such a good sleep. Are you going to be a good goat for me?"

Sarah Masters lives in York and teaches English for Speakers of Other Languages. Her tiny stories have appeared in Full House Literary, Flashflood, Shooter Flash, Pure Slush, and Chewin' The Fat.

www.twitter.com/serreyjma

There's A Possum In My Garden

Sandra Morgan

Old Yiska had been predicting a twister for weeks. Smell it in the air, he said. There he sat on his dusty porch day after day, staring up at the shifting heavens or watching the gum trees' airy heads swishing around in the rising wind.

No-one knew when Yiska first came over from Kiowa, but it had been plain for a while he'd taken a trip back there in his head and never come back, so folks would smile patronisingly at the crazy old Navajo with his twister story, as those of a sound mind do to those without.

"She'll strip them cottonwoods clean. Yup," he said, big head bobbing on his scrawny neck, white hair wisping round it like cobwebs.

"Them's gum trees, you old fart. New Zealand don't have cottonwoods, how many times do I have to tell you," barked his son - a mite unkindly, a mite unnecessary, I thought.

Still Yiska sat gazing upwards day after day, creaking out front in his rocking chair.

"Yup. She's a'comin' today," he told me that last afternoon when I stopped by with eight year old Molly to drop in some of her Mom's boysenberry muffins.

He clutched my arm. "You go shut Janie and l'il Molly sunshine up safe with you." He bestowed an adoring, toothy smile upon my daughter. "An' don't you be afright none, honey."

Molly beamed back, never seeming to mind Yiska's gap teeth like weathered tombstones. The two of them had hit it off right from the start. He was a scary old guy with slanting coal-black eyes, but Molly always let him hold her hand, letting it rest in his arthritic claw long as he wanted.

Soon as she'd been old enough to understand, he'd spun her stories about his past lives, captivating her with magical drawings: owls and eagles, fairies and hobgoblins, a Navajo Princess or two. She was the only kid in preschool more conversant with reincarnation than Peppa Pig.

The twister hit around seven, swooping in from an inky-black sky like some malevolent bird of prey bent on death and destruction. Some sixth sense had made me heed Yiska's warning and take Janie and Molly into our cellar in the nick of time, and my last sight through a rattling window was all hell breaking loose and the old-timer being swirled aloft in his rocking chair.

Stripped the gum trees clean that twister did, just like he said.

And that was the last anyone saw of Yiska.

We buried our dead, mourned lost souls, helped neighbours patch up their lives.

The seasons turned with comforting familiarity, often the customary four in one day, a polar vortex or two in winter.

And no twisters. hat we thought was forever still felt fragile, but slowly we came to believe that Yiska's twister, as it became known, had been a one-off.

Molly had just turned nine when the possum turned up in our garden.

"It's Yiska," she said, as matter-of-factly as if it were her best friend Ruby Moon.

We got used to the critter watching us from the heights of the ribbonwood tree or skulking around the garden, keeping its distance, but not too much. In between it sat looking up at the sky. Reminded me of those pictures you see of a star-gazing hare.

Now, normally you wouldn't get anywhere near a possum. Cute they might look, but over here they're classed as vermin. Sure you get your possum lovers. Me, I'm not one of them. I've got a family and Jake the cat with a cat flap. Cornered, possums get vicious, all razor-sharp teeth and claws, well-equipped to shred human flesh to ribbons.

So it's a sturdy piece of two-by-two with a large nail in the end. Sorry, possum lovers.

Duly armed, I was readying myself for carnage when Janie screamed and grabbed a carving knife. What the hell, I'm thinking. Then I saw why and my blood ran cold.

At the foot of the ribbonwood, our precious daughter was hunkered down beside the possum with its paw in her hand, her face only inches from the creature's, gazing right into its eyes. I experienced a surreal moment of clarity - my kid's communing with a possum; yep, that's right, a FERAL possum, folks.

I crept down the garden with my two-by-two, Janie behind with her knife.

"It's Yiska," Molly declared like before, as the creature lifted its head back and began to gaze skywards with slanting coal-black eyes that suddenly looked strangely familiar.

I forgot the intended bludgeoning and let my hand with its cudgel hang limply at my side, because, hell ... for a moment, there I was questioning my disbelief in reincarnation, because I could have sworn ...

Next minute, that sixth sense was back, stronger than before, and I was heedful of it like before, pulling Janie and Molly into the cellar just in the nick of time as all hell broke loose above.

Stripped those gum trees clean again.

We buried our dead, mourned for lost souls, helped neighbours piece their lives and homes back together.

Nowadays, with time moved on, I carry a deep well of gratitude around in the region of my heart, and there's not a day passes when I don't keep a lookout for a certain possum.

Conversing with one isn't something I ever felt a need for in former days, but nowadays a thank you seems in order.

Sandra's love of writing has seen her stories and serials appear in women's magazines and anthologies, along with some competition successes. Her two adventurous sons and six grandchildren, two of them Kiwi, provide endless inspiration for storylines. She lives between Bristol and Bath.

SOAKING WET

Denarii Peters

I never did like it when they came in threes. Even when my heart was happy it was too much work - all that torturing and drowning - and when the situation was like this...

I tried again to be heard. I was supposed to be in charge. I was the one who could tell if the accused was a servant of the devil or a foolish old crone. It was my decision to try by water or destroy by fire.

"Sit down. Stop shouting. Everyone will get their chance to speak. But it must be one at a time. Otherwise how can my clerk possibly list all your accusations?"

"They're not accusations. They're true."

A rumble of agreement followed the baker's words. He was a bruiser, arms as thick as his head. And one of the three was his own wife, though she was not the one who had caught my eye.

"We're wasting time. We brought you here to burn 'em." He was playing to the gallery, enjoying the moment, his wife too frightened even to sob let alone protest her innocence. And I had seen enough women exactly like her to know she was innocent. I wondered which of the other women in the crowd the baker had chosen to replace her.

It was time I cleared the room, time for the charade to begin. I nodded to my clerk and Simon got to his feet.

"The Witchfinder is ready to start. He will give his verdicts in two days' time. You will all disperse and leave this to us."

Grumbling, they shuffled out. They had hoped for more - a bit of blood, a request for tinder - but they didn't need to be so impatient. All that would follow.

The baker's wife collapsed into the arms of her companions. Perhaps she had thought he would relent when he saw me, realise it had all gone too far. If so, she had clung to a false hope.

I gave her to Simon, so enthusiastic, so eager for a victim of his own. He had not yet discovered torture is such a boring occupation.

And, worse still, he was now suspicious of me. He watched my every move and if I were to make a misstep along the way, give him the slightest cause, he would not hesitate to denounce me. If burning a "witch" gave pleasure to the mob, burning a witchfinder corrupted by the devil would give them ecstasy.

All had been well between us until we came to a small village and a smaller child. She was no more than seven. Her grandmother was the one on trial but, as is often the case, one burning is never enough. The child had the mark of a dog bite on her leg but those around her claimed it was the mark of the devil. I could not save her.

When I slept that night I saw her eyes, not accusing but terrified. My nightmare became a parade of horror, all the faces of the ones I had condemned. Not all had been women. There was the young man who had shouted defiance from the midst of the flames... until his cries became howls. He had taken a long time to die. I knew why. The villagers had steeped some of the tinder so that it smouldered. More heat, less flame.

I had become a hollow shell, too afraid to stand up, too afraid to leave my robes behind, too afraid of the accusations which could be levelled against me. So I did the work. But with every false verdict I found the words more difficult and every night I suffered my own torture.

Now there was this young woman, her hair the same raven black, her eyes the same deep green as the girl in the village. They could have been mother and daughter. Would it end my nightmares if I could find a way save her?

Simon's interrogation of the baker's wife went awry. She died by his hand but the mob tied her to the stake and burned her anyway. The other two verdicts could not be delayed much longer. I decided we should swim them.

Tied hand and foot, gagged to prevent the speaking of spells, they would be thrown into the river. If they drowned, they'd be given a Christian funeral. If they floated, they'd be dried then burned.

I saw to the knots myself. Risking everything, I whispered into her ear, "The rope is slack. Wriggle free but do not surface. Swim as far as you can underwater. I will distract the mob."

She held still as I tied the same loose knots on the other woman. But my plan for her was different.

Into the water, thrown from the bridge, shouts obscuring the splashes... I knew what would happen. It is human to struggle. My accusing finger pointed to the floating rope and the choking victim. The plan worked. No-one looked for the one who surely must have drowned. Her innocence would be her reward, an early entry into Heaven.

I'll leave Simon to take care of the drying and the burning. I've done my duty and someone has to see if it's possible to gather the corpse from the water.

Racing away downstream I look for her. She can't have swum far but there is no sign. The banks are silent, the thick reed beds undisturbed.

I stumble on blinded by tears. I have failed. Something must have gone wrong with my knots. She has indeed died and I have once again murdered innocence.

But out in the stream there are ripples, small eddies with no current, a whirlpool... and she springs from the water, soaking wet but so very alive.

I fall into her arms and hear strange words. We rise up above the river and as we fly away from the village I realise the truth.

Only a witch cannot drown.

Denarii Peters was born in the north-west of England but now lives in the county of Lincolnshire. A former primary school teacher, she spends her days writing stories and drinking a lot of coffee. In the last eighteen months she has concentrated on shorter pieces, achieving longlist or better in over 40 competitions across the world, including four third places, one second and two winning stories. This has resulted in 20 of her pieces being published in various anthologies both in print and on line.

Sixty Four Squares And The End Of The World

Coltrane Rogers

It's Patrick's move. James sits opposite him, gnawing his nails faster than a hungry beaver in a logging camp. He's down material and losing violently. Patrick shows no expression and takes the bishop with the calm of a midnight tide.

"Why is it I'm always losing when we play chess?" asks James. "I haven't beaten you once in... how many games?"

"I'll give it to you straight. I'm a magician of sorts. Your move."

"Right," says James, scanning the board. "And you perform in a circus, or do you attend birthday parties, too?"

"Neither. I was a clown once in an event, but too many kids. Too much screaming."

"You're a clown right now." James reroutes his knight and leans back in his chair, hiding a smile behind his fist as Patrick frowns at the board.

"Are you sure about that?"

"Sure about what?"

"That move."

"Well, no. Not anymore. What's wrong with it?" Patrick unleashes the queen on her warpath and begins the flank. "Oh, bugger. What trick was that then?"

84

"My magic isn't something easily understood."

"Oh, because pulling rabbits out from your hat is real complicated stuff."

"Actually, I tell the future."

James is holding a pawn and falters. "You what?"

"It's touch and move, by the way," Patrick says, pointing at the pawn in James' hand. "You've got to put it down."

James puts down the pawn on a square that cripples his defence. Patrick winces.

"So you're a psychic – Zoltar reanimated and in the flesh." James snatches Patrick's coat that rests on the back of his chair and pulls out his wallet. "Mine now," he says. "Didn't see that coming, did you?"

"I did actually," he says, moving a piece. "If you open it, you'll find yourself a note."

James raises an eyebrow but reluctantly does as he's told. Tucked behind a leather fold is a scrap of paper with something penned in blue ink. He takes it out and reads aloud:

"The world is going to end." He puts down the paper and scrunches it up. "Huh?"

"I couldn't bear to tell you in person. It's quite heavy news, so I decided to write it down for you instead."

"This doesn't prove anything. You're just a fraud." He folds his arms. "Is it my move?"

"It is. Ruin your position some more."

James does as he's told and leans back, satisfied with his cataclysmic move. "So you were saying the world is going to end?"

"Oh, yes. Plenty of fire and burning. All the movie stuff, but, without the heroes. None in this tale."

"Better cancel the holiday plans then."

Patrick checks his watch. "Better cancel the evening plans while you're at it. We've got five hours and twenty-two — make that twenty-one minutes left on this sweet earth."

"Before…"

"Before the asteroid hits and sends us to sleep like the dinosaurs," says Patrick. He picks up his queen and guides it across the board. James watches carefully.

"And you know all this how?"

"Like I said. I know the future. I know everything."

James giggles and says, "Now you're just blowing smoke up your own —

"Arse?" says Patrick. James pauses, holding the rook in his hand. "It's touch and move, by the way, you have to put it down."

"I know I know," he snaps, and puts down the rook on the first safe square he can find. "Anyone could've finished that sentence, it's a common phrase. Even a psychic fraud like you could get that. Here's the real test. What if I said —"

"Pink willy squabble with a side of a hollandaise sauce," says Patrick.

James gasps and holds his chest. He goes to speak, but Patrick steals his words: "How did you know I was going to say that? Tell me what I'm going to say next. You were going to say fish and chips, then sticky toffee

86

pudding with a tomato on top, now you want me out of your head. Am I right?"

James lifts his fingers to his mouth and prepares to gnaw at them, but they've already been hewed down to the stubs. He wasted them on the game of chess and didn't bother saving them for the world's end.

"Oh," mutters James, shaking his head. "Oh my. The world is really going to end..."

"Cheer up," says Patrick. "It's not all bad. I know one thing for sure."

"What's that?"

"You're going to beat me in this game."

James is shivering like a featherless chick and rocks on the chair. "What do you mean?" he asks.

"I resign," says Patrick, and knocks over his king, laughing.

THE DARKENING

Anne Willkins

We sit up high in the trees, just Poppa and me, swinging our legs like we ain't got a care in the world, watching the Blackness come and snuff out the Sun. Poppa says because the Sun's real old it takes an age for darkness to snuff out all the candles. But slowly all the light goes, and then we're just left with the one White Eye in the sky. Sometimes the Eye's all open, watching us, other times it's just a slither like its eyelid is closed and it's half asleep. Tonight, it must be interested in what we're doing, cos' it's all wide-eyed. I know that means the wolves are going to be playing up again, singing to it; and the seas are going to be showing off, lapping high on our shores.

"It's watching us tonight, Poppa." I point to the White Eye.

"Aye, we better show it somethin' then, eh?" And I hear the smile in his voice.

There ain't anyone like my Poppa in the village. He's the only one with the Gift. I hear him rubbing his hands together, getting them warm. "You ready, Pip?" he asks. His face is drenched in the white light of the Eye, and he looks like a little kid. A happy one.

I nod, waiting for the magic.

Poppa breathes into his hands, not too hard, not too soft. He's blowing his own little candles, but instead of blowing them out, he's lighting them up.

When he pulls his hands apart I see a tiny bubble of light peek out. It sorta floats there between his hands, just wondering what to do.

"You wanna blow it?"

And so I lean over and puff out a big one.

The little light floats away in the darkness above the trees.

"It's so pretty."

"You gotta make it not too hot with all these trees around Pip, that's the secret. Just a little bit of power. Gentle-like."

We watch the light float out across the land and head toward the sea. Just getting smaller and smaller, until it eventually disappears. Poppa's not sure if it gets swallowed by the darkness, or if it just reaches the end of our eyes.

When we both can't see it no more, he rubs his hands again. "Another?" he asks, and his eyes are all twinkly like the stars.

When we get back Mama says Poppa shouldn't be wasting his Gift on silly things for silly girls when he's got bigger things to do around the village. Poppa sighs and sets off to light any fires that have gone out or any lights that have gone.

I go with him as I don't like being 'round Mama when she's got the temper about her.

Poppa rolls up a little ball of light and holds it in his hands as we go walkin' and knocking on people's doors.

There's only one house that needs a new ball of light. The woman hands Poppa her lantern and her little light ball looks all sad like it's dying. It's not even floating, it's just sitting on the bottom of the lantern, like it's given up. Poppa pulls it out and rubs it between his fingers and it gets to be all glowing and happy again. He puts it back in the lantern where it floats around.

"There you go," he says, handing the woman back her lantern and she doesn't even say thanks as she closes the door on us.

I look around our little village. All the little lights dotted on the hillside, all the fires in the homes keeping people warm. That's all thanks to my Poppa.

"She shud've thanked you."

"Aye, people forget." And that's all he says, but his eyes don't twinkle the way they should.

I'm thinkin' maybe the White Eye in the sky wasn't happy with somethin' it saw that night, cos' it wasn't too long afterward that the thankless woman we visited got sick.

Poppa, being Poppa, still went to her house, made sure her fires and lights were all on.

And then Poppa got sick.

He normally made light from his hands, but this time he was coughing up little light balls from his throat, and when he got the fever he was burning up so much Mama thought the house might flame up. We had to drench him in water.

"He's goin' to be alright, isn't he Ma?" I asked as his skin flushed bright red.

But she only answered with tears.

All the lights and fires in our village began to dwindle, and people started knocking on our door. Some of them were all nice as pie, bringing their half-dead lanterns asking if Poppa could just blow a little life into their ball of light, and some were all angry, shouting for Poppa to get up and light their fires and lights.

We turned them all away and Mama held Poppa's hands and mopped his brow and sang sweet songs to him while the light faded.

Two nights later the Blackness came and snuffed out Poppa's candles. It didn't do it all slow like it does with the sun, it just came and with one black breath, he was gone.

I'm thinking the Blackness must've taken some of Mama's light too when it visited, because she's all cold now, and something in her eyes has died.

One by one, all the lights and fires in our village died.

And then there was only darkness.

The thing is the darkness had been here all along. In our people. It took Poppa's death to show me that.

I'm thinking all this as I'm sitting on our tree, with the White Eye watching me. I'm thinking all this as I rub my hands together and feel something burn.

And I'm thinking all this as I decide to keep my little Gift to myself, for a bit longer.

Anne Wilkins lives in New Zealand with her husband, two teenage daughters, and her imagination (it's big and sometimes nasty). She is a primary school teacher but was previously a lawyer specialising in family law. Anne has written two children's novels (currently unpublished) and many short stories, some of which are published in various anthologies. Her love of writing is fuelled by coffee, reading and hope. She was most recently the winner of the Cambridge Autumn Festival Short Story competition in New Zealand.

www.facebook.com/anne.w.wilson.1

www.ingramcontent.com/pod-product-compliance
Lightning Source LLC
Chambersburg PA
CBHW021128130626
46554CB00002B/911